The
MAGICAL WORLD
of
STREGA NONA

Merry Christmas, Nonni + Nash

The MAGICAL WORLD of STREGA NONA

xxx

A TREASURY

BY

TOMIE dePAOLA

Tomie 2015

*To Nonni & Nash
Merry Christmas
Hope you enjoy this
book as much as
we do!!
XXOO
Lynn &
Pete*

Nancy Paulsen Books ◉ An Imprint of Penguin Group (USA)

NANCY PAULSEN BOOKS
Published by the Penguin Group
Penguin Group (USA) LLC
375 Hudson Street
New York, NY 10014

USA | Canada | UK | Ireland | Australia
New Zealand | India | South Africa | China
penguin.com
A Penguin Random House Company

Library of Congress Cataloging-in-Publication Data
DePaola, Tomie, 1934- author, illustrator.
[Folk tales. Selections]
The magical world of Strega Nona : a treasury / Tomie dePaola.
pages cm
Summary: "A treasury of six previously published stories about Strega Nona, the 'grandmother witch,'
and her sidekick, the bumbling Big Anthony, plus new material including introductions, a map, recipes,
and an original lullaby (with sheet music and a CD)"—Provided by publisher.
[1. Folklore—Italy.] I. Title.   PZ8.1.D43Mag 2015   398.20945'02—dc23   2014044928

Manufactured in China by RR Donnelley Asia Printing Solutions Ltd.
ISBN 978-0-399-17345-5
1 3 5 7 9 10 8 6 4 2

Design by Marikka Tamura.

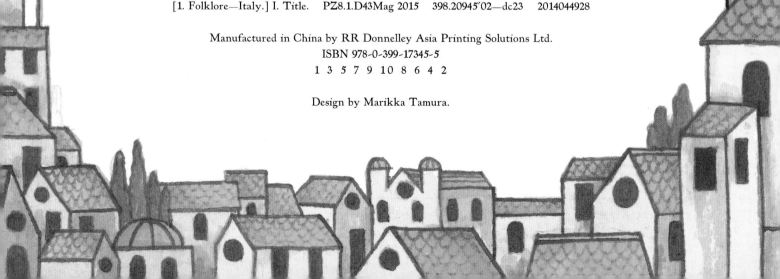

CONTENTS

Everyone always wants to know just how Strega Nona came about. Many people think that she is a character in Italian folklore, and I even have people telling me that they are "so happy to see the Strega Nona stories in a book."

In fact, years ago, right after *Strega Nona* was first published in 1975, I was about to speak at a conference, and this rather impressive woman with jet-black hair ran up to me. Wearing a black dress with a red flower pinned to her shoulder, she looked like an Italian opera star—a diva.

"Tomie dePaola!" she bellowed (pronouncing my name correctly!). She grabbed me, pressed me to her bosom (she was taller than me), and said, "Thank God, someone is doing the Strega Nona stories again!"

That took me by surprise. Had my Italian collective unconscious channeled Strega Nona, or was she a part of my imagination? I thought I had *invented* her. So, I delved through as much Italian folklore as I could, and lo and behold—NO STREGA NONA—ANYWHERE.

So, here's the real scoop on how Strega Nona came about . . .

In the early 1970s, I was teaching in the theater department at what is now Colby-Sawyer College in New Hampshire. My books were beginning to get noticed, so my editor at Prentice-Hall (now Simon & Schuster), Ellen Roberts, suggested that I look into retelling and illustrating a folktale.

Well, some months before, at a required weekly college faculty meeting (I always sat in the back row with a legal pad and doodled—the administration thought I was taking notes), I was, as usual, doodling. I was obsessed with the Italian commedia dell'arte character Punchinello. So many of my doodles were of him—big nose, big chin.

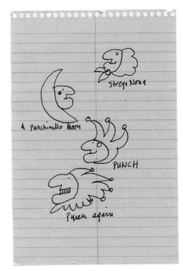

On my pad, I drew the profile, but suddenly I found I had drawn a headscarf. I put in the eye and the smiling mouth and continued to draw a little chubby body, complete with long skirt and apron. And I scribbled the words "Strega Nona" next to the drawing.

I was tickled pink. She was so cute, so Italian, and I thought I might be able to use her in a book someday. I pinned the doodle up on my studio wall.

Back to Ellen Roberts and her suggestion that I retell a folktale. "What was one of your favorite folktales when you were a child?" she asked.

"The porridge pot story," I answered immediately.

"Why don't you reread it in a version that's in the public domain and see if you're interested enough in it to retell it," Ellen said.

So, I reread the story. But I didn't really like it. Suddenly, LIGHTBULB TIME!

Maybe I could change *porridge* to *pasta* and use my little Strega Nona (who was already "telling" me who she was).

I called Ellen to ask if it was legal to retell a story.

"Of course," she said, "as long as the story is in the public domain." (A story in the public domain is a story for which the copyright has expired or lapsed. Public domain stories are usually very old.)

So, I started working on the text for *Strega Nona*.

The original manuscript, written by hand on a yellow legal pad, is at the Kerlan Children's Literature Research Collections at the University of Minnesota in Minneapolis. (Children's book writers and illustrators give their book manuscript materials and illustration materials to the Kerlan to safely preserve forever. Similar repositories are at the University of Connecticut and at the University of Southern Mississippi.) If you ever get a chance to see the original manuscript, you'll notice that Big Anthony was originally a GIRL named Concetta! But I felt that the world did not need one more not-too-bright servant girl in folklore, so I crossed out "Concetta" and wrote instead, "Big Anthony, who did not pay attention."

One more controversy.

"Why," many Italians and Italian Americans ask me, "is *Nona* spelled with one *n* instead of two?" (The Italian word for "grandmother" is *nonna*.)

Strega Nona is Calabrese, like my ancestors. Calabria is in the toe of the boot of Italy. As far as my relatives told me, *nona* is a slang spelling for "granny" or "grandma," which, after all, is spelled differently than "grandmother."

And, on top of it all, Nona is her NAME. I settled that in *Strega Nona: Her Story*, I hope.

But the truth of the matter is that Strega Nona *is* bigger than life, and she certainly changed mine.

After all, I tell audiences, "Strega Nona built my swimming pool." And finally, maybe you'll notice that Strega Nona looks a tiny bit different in the first book than she does later on. Well, as I got to *know* her better, I began to draw her better!

Tomie

MAP LEGEND

A: Nona Concetta's cottage

B: town where Strega Amelia lives

C: road from the north (Big Anthony)

D: bakery (Bambolona's father)

E: convent school

F: convent

G: Church of San Francesco di Paola

H: priest's house

I: mayor's house

J: town hall

K: gates of the village

L: gallery

M: Chapel of San Tommasino

N: houses of the townspeople

O: town square (piazza)

P: fountain

Q: Strega Nona's house and goat shed

This is the book that started it all. From a doodle of Strega Nona to the idea of retelling my favorite childhood folktale, "The Porridge Pot," with the porridge changing to pasta, Strega Nona was born. I had no idea that this little old Italian woman who had magical powers and a profile that resembled Punchinello would ever live in more than one book—let alone Big Anthony!

In the original folktale, the old woman with the magic porridge pot has a dim servant girl who misuses the magic, but that didn't sit well with me. So I changed the character to a young man who "didn't pay attention," and called him Big Anthony. Anthony is my middle name. I kept the original old woman, who became Strega Nona, which means "Grandma Witch."

Often, my young readers will ask me if anyone inspired Big Anthony. I answer that I made him look a little like my cousin Frankie. At first my cousin Frankie wasn't very happy about that, but when *Strega Nona* was chosen as a Caldecott Honor Book in 1976, he began to brag to everyone, "My cousin Tomie used me as his inspiration for Big Anthony." I'm lucky he didn't ask me to share my royalties with him!

I really enjoyed doing the illustrations for the first *Strega Nona*. I loved doing the rooftops of the Italian buildings of the Middle Ages. I was able to use my love for the early artists—Giotto, Cimabue, Duccio, and Fra Angelico—as my inspiration. And I always have loved the way the Japanese woodcut artist Hokusai depicted water and waves. That was my inspiration for the tons of pasta threatening to cover the town.

Tomie

an original tale written and illustrated by Tomie dePaola

Strega Nona

For Franny and Fuffy

In a town in Calabria, a long time ago, there lived an old lady everyone called Strega Nona, which meant "Grandma Witch."

Although all the people in town talked about her in whispers, they all went to see her if they had troubles. Even the priest and the sisters of the convent went, because Strega Nona *did* have a magic touch.

She could cure a headache, with oil and water and a hairpin.

She made special potions for the girls who wanted husbands.

And she was very good at getting rid of warts.

But Strega Nona was getting old, and she needed someone to help her keep her little house and garden, so she put up a sign in the town square.

And Big Anthony, who didn't pay attention, went to see her.

"Anthony," said Strega Nona, "you must sweep the house and wash the dishes. You must weed the garden and pick the vegetables. You must feed the goat and milk her. And you must fetch the water. For this, I will give you three coins and a place to sleep and food to eat."

"Oh, *grazie*," said Big Anthony.

"The one thing you must never do," said Strega Nona, "is touch the pasta pot. It is very valuable and I don't let anyone touch it!"

"Oh, *si*, yes," said Big Anthony.

And so the days went by. Big Anthony did his work and Strega Nona met with the people who came to see her for headaches and husbands and warts.

Big Anthony had a nice bed to sleep in next to the goat shed, and he had food to eat.

One evening when Big Anthony was milking the goat, he heard Strega Nona singing. Peeking in the window, he saw Strega Nona standing over the pasta pot.

She sang,

> Bubble, bubble, pasta pot,
>
> Boil me some pasta, nice and hot,
>
> I'm hungry and it's time to sup,
>
> Boil enough pasta to fill me up.

And the pasta pot bubbled and boiled and was suddenly filled with steaming hot pasta.

Then Strega Nona sang,

> Enough, enough, pasta pot,
>
> I have my pasta, nice and hot,
>
> So simmer down my pot of clay,
>
> Until I'm hungry another day.

"How wonderful!" said Big Anthony. "That's a magic pot for sure!"

And Strega Nona called Big Anthony in for supper.

But too bad for Big Anthony, because he didn't get to see
Strega Nona blow three kisses to the magic pasta pot.

And this is what happened.

The next day when Big Anthony went to the town square to fetch the water, he told everyone about the pasta pot.

And naturally everyone laughed at him, because it sounded so silly—a pot that cooked all by itself.

"You'd better go and confess to the priest, Big Anthony," they said. "Such a lie!"

And Big Anthony was angry and that wasn't a very good thing to be.

"I'll show them!" he said to himself. "Someday I will get the pasta pot and make it cook! And then *they'll* be sorry."

That day came sooner than even Big Anthony would have thought, because two days later Strega Nona said to Big Anthony, "Anthony, I must go over the mountain to the next town to see my friend, Strega Amelia. Sweep the house and weed the garden. Feed the goat and milk her and for your lunch, there are some bread and cheese in the cupboard. And remember, don't touch the pasta pot."

"Oh, yes—yes—Strega Nona," said Big Anthony.
But inside he was thinking, *My chance has come!*

As soon as Strega Nona was out of sight, Big Anthony went inside, pulled the pasta pot off the shelf, and put it on the floor.

"Now, let's see if I can remember the words," said Big Anthony.
And Big Anthony sang,

> Bubble, bubble, pasta pot,
>
> Boil me some pasta, nice and hot,
>
> I'm hungry and it's time to sup,
>
> Boil enough to fill me up.

And sure enough, the pot bubbled and boiled and began to fill up with pasta.

"Aha!" said Big Anthony, and he ran to the town square, jumped on the fountain, and shouted, "Everyone get forks and plates and platters and bowls. Pasta for all at Strega Nona's house. Big Anthony has made the magic pasta pot work."

Of course everyone laughed, but ran home to get forks and plates and platters and bowls, and sure enough, when they got to Strega Nona's the pasta pot was so full it was beginning to overflow.

Big Anthony was a hero!

He scooped out pasta and filled the plates
and platters and bowls.

There was more than enough for all the townspeople, including the priest and the sisters from the convent.

And some people came back for two and three helpings, but the pot was never empty.

When all had had their fill, Big Anthony sang,
Enough, enough, my pasta pot,
I have my pasta nice and hot,
So simmer down, my pot of clay,
Until I'm hungry another day.
But, alas, he did not blow the three kisses!

He went outside and to the applause of the crowd, Big Anthony took a bow.

He was so busy listening to compliments from everyone that he didn't notice the pasta pot was still bubbling and boiling, until a sister from the convent said, "Oh, Big Anthony, look!"

And pasta was pouring out of the pot all over the floor of Strega Nona's house and was coming out the door!

Big Anthony rushed in and shouted the magic words again,
but the pot kept bubbling.

He took the pot off the floor, but pasta kept pouring from it.

Big Anthony grabbed a cover and put it on the pot and sat on it.

But the pasta raised the cover, and Big Anthony as well,
and spilled on the floor of Strega Nona's house.

"Stop!" yelled Big Anthony.

But the pasta did not stop and if someone hadn't grabbed poor Big Anthony, the pasta would have covered him up. The pasta had all but filled the little house.

Out of the windows and through the doors came the pasta and the pot kept right on bubbling.

The townspeople began to worry.

"Do something, Big Anthony," they shouted.

Big Anthony sang the magic song again but without the three kisses it did no good!

By this time the pasta was on its way down the road and all the people were running to keep ahead of it.

"We must protect our town from the pasta," shouted the mayor.
"Get mattresses, tables, doors—anything to make a barricade."

But even that didn't work. The pot kept bubbling
and the pasta kept coming!

"We are lost," said the people, and the priest and the sisters of the convent began praying. "The pasta will cover our town," they cried.

And it certainly would have, had Strega Nona not come down the road, home from her visit.

She didn't have to look twice to know what had happened.

She sang the magic song and blew the three kisses and with
a sputter the pot stopped boiling and the pasta came to a halt.

"Oh, *grazie*—thank you, thank you, Strega Nona," the people cried.

But then they turned on poor Big Anthony.

"String him up," the men of the town shouted.

"Now, wait," said Strega Nona. "The punishment must fit the crime." And she took a fork from a lady standing nearby and held it out to Big Anthony.

"All right, Anthony, you wanted pasta from my magic pasta pot," Strega Nona said, "and *I* want to sleep in my little bed tonight. So start eating."

And he did—poor Big Anthony.

I never intended to do more than one book about Strega Nona. But everyone seemed to love this little "Strega" so much, I wrote a second, third, and then a fourth book about her and Big Anthony. I added the baker's daughter and named her Bambolona. Those three books were *Big Anthony and the Magic Ring*, *Strega Nona's Magic Lessons*, and *Merry Christmas, Strega Nona*. People seemed to love them, too.

I often tell people that I don't sit down and try to think about another Strega Nona idea. She, herself, comes to me and "whispers" in my ear, "Do I have a story for you!" It happens when I least expect it. So, that's how *Strega Nona Meets Her Match* came about.

Strega Nona went to visit her friend Strega Amelia in the first book. That's when Big Anthony messed around with the pasta pot. But then, Strega Nona *said to me*, "You won't believe what happened when my old friend Strega Amelia came to visit me!"

Of course, Big Anthony still doesn't pay attention!

Tomie

Tomie dePaola

STREGA NONA
Meets Her Match

For my wonderful friend
Mary Ann Esposito
and *her* good friend
"Nellie Cucina"

Nothing much happened in the little town in Calabria where Strega Nona lived. At least, nothing had happened since Big Anthony had left Strega Nona's magic pasta pot alone.

Bambolona, the baker's daughter, was learning how to become a *strega* too. She listened to everything Strega Nona told her. Not like Big Anthony, who never listened to anyone. Bambolona kept everything running smoothly. So life was peaceful in Strega Nona's little house on the hill.

Then one day a letter arrived for Strega Nona. It was from Strega Amelia, who lived on the other side of the mountain.

"Cara Strega Nona," the letter read. "I would like to pay you a visit. Would next week be convenient? Please let me know. *Amore e baci"*—Love and kisses—"Strega Amelia."

Strega Nona sat right down and wrote a letter telling Strega Amelia to come as soon as possible.

Big Anthony and Bambolona helped Strega Nona get the house ready. They swept and polished, and shook out the sheets.

"I have so few visitors to stay, my children," Strega Nona told them. "It will be wonderful to have company. And Big Anthony, please try to behave and pay attention while Strega Amelia is here."

"Ah, *sì*, Strega Nona," Big Anthony answered. "I'll be so good you won't recognize me!"

"I'll believe that when I see it," Bambolona whispered to Strega Nona.

"Shh. Now be nice, Bambolona," Strega Nona whispered back.

"*Ciao, cara,*" Strega Amelia called, as she reached the top of the hill.

"Ah, my dear friend," Strega Nona said. *"Avanti, avanti"*—Come in, come in.

The two *streghe* sat right down, put their heads together, and talked and laughed and gossiped until Bambolona came and stood in the doorway.

"Ah now, dear Amelia," Strega Nona said. "Bambolona has made a wonderful supper for us. *Mangia!*"—Eat!

The next morning Strega Nona was busy helping the townspeople who came to her to cure their headaches, to find husbands, and to get rid of warts.

Strega Amelia watched. "Goodness," she said to Big Anthony. "Strega Nona has *un buon numero di clienti*"—a great many customers. "Is it always this way?"

"Oh, *sì*," Big Anthony answered. "Sometimes it's even busier than this!"

"Per l'amor di Dio!"—for goodness' sake!—Strega Amelia exclaimed. "I see she still uses the old-fashioned ways too. Hmm, I'll have to think about this."

The next day Strega Amelia went home. "*Arrivederci*, Strega
Nona. Good-bye, Bambolona. Good-bye, Big Anthony," Strega
Amelia called as she went down the hill.

"*Addio*, Strega Amelia"—Farewell—the three called back.

A week later, when Big Anthony was feeding the goat, he looked out over the hillside and saw several carts coming into town. "Bambolona," he called. "Come and look."

"Why, it looks like…It is!" Bambolona said. "It's Strega Amelia. What's she up to?"

"Let's ask Strega Nona," Big Anthony said.

"No. Let's go down and find out," Bambolona said. And they crept down the hill to see for themselves.

They were back in no time.

"Strega Nona, Strega Nona," Bambolona and Big Anthony called, all out of breath.

"What is it, my children?" Strega Nona asked.

"You'll never guess. Read this!" Bambolona handed Strega Nona a handbill.

OPENING TOMORROW

STREGA AMELIA'S HELPFUL SERVICES

Husbands found for young ladies,
headaches cured,
warts removed; other remedies
Latest scientific equipment
FREE sweets and coffee with every visit

"Well," Strega Nona said. "I don't think there's anything to worry about."

But Strega Nona was wrong.

One by one the townspeople started to go to Strega Amelia.
Everyone got *dolci*—sweets—and *cappuccino* for paying a visit, and
indeed she had the latest scientific equipment—strange-looking
machines that did all kinds of things. The lines of people grew
longer and longer. Strega Nona had met her match.

Finally one morning not a single person came to Strega Nona's house. And it was that way for days and days. Poor Strega Nona!

After three weeks, Strega Nona called in Bambolona and Big Anthony.

"My children, I must talk with you. *Mia borsa*"—my purse— "is empty. I won't be able to pay you anymore. I'm afraid there is no work here. You must go down to the town and see what you can find." And Strega Nona went back into her little house.

The next morning Bambolona was there as usual. "My papa can use some help in the bakery, Strega Nona, so I'll be all right. And I'll be able to come by a few days a week to help you too!"

"Ah, my sweet Bambolona. You are so good," Strega Nona told her. "But what about our Big Anthony?"

"Here he comes now," Bambolona said.

"Oh, Strega Nona, Bambolona, you'll never guess! I have a new job!" Big Anthony shouted out, all smiles.

"You don't have to sound so happy about it." Bambolona scowled.

"Now, now," Strega Nona said. "Tell us, Big Anthony. What is it?"

"I'm going to work for Strega Amelia!" Big Anthony exclaimed.

"You're *what!*" Bambolona screamed.

"Stop! Stop!" yelled Big Anthony.

"Yes, Bambolona, stop!" Strega Nona said. "I think that is wonderful, Big Anthony. When do you start?"

"Today, Strega Nona. I have to run there right now. Wish me luck!" Big Anthony said, as he turned and ran down the hill.

"Buona fortuna"—Good luck—Strega Nona called after him.

"How could he? *How could he!* The big ungrateful traitor!" Bambolona fumed.

"Oh, Big Anthony. You are such a help to me!" Strega Amelia exclaimed, as Big Anthony followed her around doing exactly what he was told.

He polished the husband-and-wife machine.

He filled up the wart-cream jars.

He stirred the hair restorer in the big pot on the stove.

"Well, Big Anthony, business is booming," Strega Amelia remarked one morning. "I had a feeling that people would like the modern ways, especially my headache machine. And now that you have been here a few weeks, I'm going to leave you in charge for a few days while I go over the mountain to get the rest of my equipment. Now sit down and listen carefully while I explain how to run everything."

Big Anthony smiled. He was in charge.

The first day he ran the husband-and-wife machine backward.

The second day he confused the wart cream with the hair restorer.

Things weren't going too well. On the third day, the mayor arrived.

"*Buon giorno*, Signor Mayor," Big Anthony said. "What can I do for you?"

"Oh, Big Anthony," the mayor groaned. "I have a terrible headache. Strega Amelia's machine is a wonder. Strap me in."

Big Anthony settled the mayor in the headache machine and picked up the diagram that showed how to work it. He looked at the diagram. It was very complicated. (And it was upside down!)

The next morning all the townspeople were back at Strega
Nona's. The mayor was the first in line.

"Bambolona," Strega Nona said, "run down and get Big
Anthony. We need him."

When the carts came over the mountain with Strega Amelia in
front, the townspeople were waiting at the town gate.

"I'm sorry," the mayor told Strega Amelia, "but we all agree that we prefer the old ways. Our own Strega Nona is enough for us. We hope you have no hard feelings."

"*Arrivederci*, Strega Amelia," Strega Nona said. "I'm sorry it didn't work out for you."

"*Arrivederci*, Strega Nona," Strega Amelia said. "I must admit, I am surprised. Everything was going so well. And as for your Big Anthony, I know you've had trouble with him, but I must tell you I couldn't have done it without him. He was such a big help."

"He certainly was," Strega Nona said with a smile.

Strega Nona was becoming quite famous! And when people become famous, all kinds of stories start going around about them. Most of these stories aren't true. It was the same thing for Strega Nona.

People, even older than me at the time, started telling me that their grandmothers had told them the Strega Nona stories. One person even told me that Strega Nona did not come from Calabria; she came from Tuscany. How could this be? I made Strega Nona up out of my own head. It was true that she was a little bit like my Italian grandmother in the way she did "magic." My grandmother did cure headaches for the ladies in the neighborhood with water, oil, and a hairpin like Strega Nona. And I knew other Italian ladies had similar "powers," but I began to think that somewhere along the way, maybe when I was really young, I had *heard* stories about a character called Strega Nona. I began to research Italian folktales, but all my hard work didn't turn up ANY character named Strega Nona, and the only story I told that was similar to an old folktale ("The Porridge Pot") was the first book.

I didn't have to wait long. Sure enough, Strega Nona whispered, "Start writing and I will tell you my story myself, to put an end to all these rumors going around about me."

I did what I was told. And I loved drawing Strega Nona when she was a little girl.

(I also wrote *Big Anthony: His Story*, but there wasn't room for that book in this treasury. Sorry.)

Tomie

STREGA NONA
Her Story
as told to
Tomie dePaola

For Connie, Mel, Tom, Alan, Jon, Gary, Wendy, Josette,
Julie, Mary L., Leif, Steve, Cary, Ricia, Mary G., Mary C.,
and all the others at The Children's Theatre Company in
Minneapolis, for helping bring Strega Nona and her
friends to life on the stage.

It all began one night a long time ago, in a little village in the hills of Calabria, in the country now known as Italy. Almost everyone was fast asleep.

The weather was fierce that dark night. The wind blew and blew. A cold rain fell. And a baby was about to be born.

"Oh, my poor wife," Giuseppe, the young husband, said to Zia Rosa, who was there to help. "Every child of ours was brought into the world by Grandma Concetta. But with this terrible weather, how will she be able to come down from her little house on the hill?"

Hours passed. The wind blew harder. More rain fell. Still the baby didn't come. "Where is that baby?" Giuseppe asked.

Zia Rosa lit a candle. "Perhaps it is waiting," she answered.

"For what?" Giuseppe asked.

"For ME!" cried Grandma Concetta, bursting through the doorway on a gust of wind. "No grandchild of mine can be born without ME!" Taking off her cloak and rolling up her sleeves, she headed for the bedroom. "Follow me, Rosa. Now the baby will come!"

And sure enough, a baby girl was born in no time at all.

"Ah," said Grandma Concetta, looking down at the new *bambina*, "she shall be called Nona. And she will become a strega."

As soon as little Nona could walk, Grandma Concetta took her along when she gathered herbs and weeds for her lotions and potions. Grandma Concetta was a strega, and all the villagers came to her for cures and advice on many things.

"Ah, Nonalina, here is *rosmarino*—rosemary. Very good for growing hair, especially on bald heads. Also excellent as furniture polish.

"And here is *aglio selvatico*—wild garlic. The only thing for an upset stomach. Come along. Let's see what else we can find."

By the end of their walk, Grandma Concetta's basket would be filled to overflowing.

When little Nona was old enough to go to school, she was sent
to study with the sisters of the convent. There she met little Amelia,
and they became best friends right away. Nona helped Amelia with
her lessons, especially spelling and writing. And Amelia, in turn, loaned
Nona her pretty hair ribbons, even though Nona didn't ask for them.

One day Amelia looked at Nona and said, "We should do something different with your hair." So Amelia curled it.

"Hmm, perhaps the braids *are* better," Amelia said.

Best of all, Nona and Amelia liked to visit Grandma Concetta. While Nona held the big book of spells and Amelia turned the pages, Grandma Concetta always said, "I knew the first time I looked at you, Nona, that one day you would become a strega. But I had no idea I would have *two* little girls to pass my magic down to. I am filled with *contentezza*—contentment."

Nona and Amelia watched Grandma Concetta mix her lotions and potions. They listened as she talked to the villagers about their troubles—headaches, warts, baldness, and other worries—and gave them her remedies, along with good advice.

And after all the villagers had gone back down the hill at the end of the day, Grandma Concetta gave the girls wonderful plates of steaming hot pasta. It appeared from her pasta pot as if by magic, and it tasted so special that Nona and Amelia always asked Grandma Concetta what her secret ingredient was. But Grandma Concetta would only smile and say nothing.

When the girls finished at the *convento,* the convent school, it was decided that they would go to the city and enter the Accademia delle Streghe—the Academy for Stregas—where they would learn the most modern ways to do magic.

Amelia loved the city—the bustle, the noise, and most of all the shopping. And she loved learning to use the Academy's machines and the new, scientific ways to do spells. "Nona," she said, "this is all so much better than the old ways Grandma Concetta uses."

But Nona missed the old spells. She didn't like the city streets, and she longed for walks in the country with Grandma Concetta, whom she missed most of all.

So Nona went home and climbed the hill to Grandma Concetta's house.

"Well, *cara mia*," Grandma Concetta said after hearing Nona's story, "the Accademia is not for everyone. I have a feeling you need to be right here with me."

So Nona began learning to be a strega from the best strega of them all—Grandma Concetta.

She learned how to mix lotions and potions. She turned the pages of the big book for Grandma Concetta. And she watched the way Grandma Concetta treated each villager who walked up the hill to ask for her help.

Every day Nona cleaned and polished Grandma Concetta's pasta pot. She knew it was magic, but Grandma Concetta never showed her how to use it. And whenever Nona asked about it, Grandma Concetta always answered, "There will be time enough, Nona. Now, here's how you make the lotion to remove warts. . . ."

"Nona! Grandma Concetta! It's Amelia, home for a visit!"

Oh, it was so good to see Amelia again. They all kissed and talked. Amelia talked the most, telling Nona and Grandma Concetta all about the machines at the Academy and the fancy scientific methods she now knew how to use.

"Did you learn any of the old spells?" Grandma Concetta asked.

"Oh, yes indeed," Amelia answered. "Watch the goat!" She opened her notebook and chanted some strange words: *capra*—goat; *tetto*—roof; and presto! With a bang and a cloud of smoke, Grandma's goat was on the roof!

"*Ecco fatto*—that's it," she exclaimed proudly. "It's a spell for Moving Things Up. We use it to put things back on shelves. Isn't that wonderful?"

"Very good, Amelia. Now will you get my goat down?" Grandma
Concetta asked. Amelia looked through her notebook. She looked and
looked. "I must have gone shopping that day," she said.

"Maybe Nona can do it," Grandma Concetta said.

Nona looked up at the roof. Then she ran into the house and came back with a bottle of olive oil. She climbed up the tree next to the little house and poured some oil on the roof. The goat slipped and slid right off!

"Oh, Nona, how marvelously clever you are," Amelia said. "But look what I have from the Academy." She opened her *borsa*—purse—and pulled out a big piece of parchment. "This is my diploma that says I am a genuine strega. Now, don't worry, Grandma Concetta, Nona. I'm not going to give you any competition," she said, laughing at her own joke. "But I am opening up business in the town on the other side of the mountain. It's much bigger and busier than our little village. And it has so many shops! You must come and see me," she told them. "Well, I'm off. *Arrivederci*, sweet Nona, sweet Grandma Concetta."

That evening, Nona and Grandma Concetta sat outside before Nona went home. Nona was very quiet.

"Nonalina, *cara*," Grandma Concetta said, "what is the matter?"

"I guess I'll never be a real strega like Amelia. I won't ever have a diploma."

"Ah," Grandma Concetta said, "you don't need a diploma to be a true strega. You already have everything you need. You have the spirit and kindness that come from the heart. And when I pass my practice over to you, I will tell you the *ingrediente segreto*—the secret ingredient. Then you will be not only a true strega, but a great one."

Years went by. One day, Grandma Concetta called Nona to her. "It's time, Nona. I am ready to retire. I am going to spend the rest of my days at the seashore, and you must take my place. You shall have my little house, my book of spells, my herbs, and my remedies.

"And in the cupboard, I have left you my pasta pot with something inside it." And with that Grandma Concetta said, "From this day forth, you shall be known as Strega Nona!"

Then she put on her cloak, picked up her bag, and started down the hill.

Nona stood in front of the little house that was now hers. She waved and waved until Grandma Concetta was out of sight. Nona wiped away a tear and walked inside. She went straight to the cupboard and looked in the pasta pot. There she found a letter.

Cara Strega Nona,

my magic pasta pot is now yours. Whenever you are hungry, sing the little song written here, and the pot will bubble and boil and fill with fresh hot pasta. When you have enough, sing the second song.

But then you must blow three kisses and the pot will stop.

For that is the INGREDIENTE SEGRETO, LOVE... It is the same with all your magic. Always LOVE!

Your Grandma Concetta

①
BUBBLE BUBBLE PASTA POT,
BOIL ME SOME PASTA,
   NICE AND HOT,
I'M HUNGRY AND IT'S
   TIME TO SUP.
BOIL ENOUGH PASTA
   TO FILL ME UP.

②
ENOUGH, ENOUGH PASTA POT,
I HAVE MY PASTA,
   NICE AND HOT,
SO SIMMER DOWN
   MY POT OF CLAY,
UNTIL I'M HUNGRY
   ANOTHER DAY.

More years passed, and Strega Nona was loved by everyone. She helped all the people who came to her with their troubles, even the priest and the sisters of the convent. She did have a magic touch.

And always, Strega Nona never forgot the *ingrediente segreto*.

Life was happy in the little house on the hill. Strega Nona kept the goat, a peacock, a rabbit, and a dove for company.

But Strega Nona was getting old, and she needed someone to help keep her little house and garden and her dear animals. So she went down to the village square and put up a sign.

The next day there was a knock on her door.

The rest is history.

One night, I was watching some very old home movies that my dad had taken of us when we went on a summer vacation to Fall River, Massachusetts. There I was with my cousin Frankie at the shore cottage of our uncle Frank (Frankie was named after him), playing in the water, learning to swim. All of a sudden, out of the cottage came my Italian grandmother in what looked like a big black dress. It was her bathing suit. She blessed herself and went into the water. Then she floated around and around. I remember telling my friend Jeannie Houdlette that my Italian "nana" went swimming. Jeannie told me that her grandmother in Maine just sat in a chair in the house and looked out the window. I felt very lucky that I had such an interesting grandmother.

I was remembering all this when those "whispers" from Strega Nona started again. "I had a bathing costume just like the one your nana wore," she told me. "I went on a vacation to the seashore, too. Let me tell you about it—and yes, Big Anthony got in trouble again!"

Look for the pictures of Strega Nona swimming. She looks just like Nana Fall-River.

♡Tomie

Tomie dePaola

STREGA NONA

Takes a Vacation

For Mario, who finally got
a dedication just for himself!

Strega Nona was having *un sogno*—a dream. She was a little girl again in her Grandma Concetta's house at the seashore.

What a wonderful time they were having!

"*Vieni*, Nonalina, *vieni*," Grandma Concetta called. "Come, Nonalina."
Strega Nona woke up. She was in her house on the hill above the little
village in Calabria.

All day long, as Strega Nona helped the villagers with their headaches, toothaches, and other worries, she kept hearing Grandma Concetta's voice from the dream.

Some of the villagers said to each other, "It looks like Strega Nona needs a vacation."

"Big Anthony," Bambolona said. "Strega Nona has something on her mind."

"I know," Big Anthony said. "She almost gave Signore Mayor the wrong remedy for his headache. That's the first time that's ever happened!"

Strega Nona looked out of her window. She was sure that she had heard Grandma Concetta calling to her.

How can that be? Strega Nona thought to herself. *Grandma Concetta has been in* cielo—heaven—*for many years. I wish I knew what the dream meant.*

That very night, Strega Nona got her answer. In another dream she was sitting just outside the little house on the hill. Opposite her was Grandma Concetta.

"Dear Nona," she said. "You've been working so hard all these years. You *must* take *una vacanza*—a vacation. Bambolona can do the daily remedies and Big Anthony can do the chores—feeding the animals, milking the goat, and looking after the house and the garden. My little seashore house is empty, just waiting for you. Come, Nona, come."

Strega Nona woke up.

"*Andrò*," she said. "I'll go!" And she fell back asleep with a big smile on her face.

The next morning she asked Big Anthony and Bambolona to come inside.

"Sit down, my children. I have some news. I'm going to take *una vacanza* at Grandma Concetta's little house by the seashore."

"Oh," said Bambolona. "When will you go?"

"The day after tomorrow," Strega Nona said.

"When will you come back?" Big Anthony asked.

"I will let you know," Strega Nona said. "I will send you a message."

"*Arrivederci*, my children," Strega Nona said. "You'll be fine, Bambolona. If you have any questions about which spells to use, look in the big book. If there are any unusual cases, just go over the mountain and ask Strega Amelia to help you." Strega Nona gave Bambolona *un bacio*—a kiss.

"Now, Big Anthony, I know you'll be a good boy and not get into any trouble. Just do everything you usually do. Help Bambolona if she asks. And remember…"

Bambolona and Big Anthony chimed in:

"DON'T TOUCH THE PASTA POT!"

They all laughed, remembering the day that Big Anthony had flooded the village with pasta!

Strega Nona gave Big Anthony *un bacio* too.

Ah, there it was, the little house at the seashore.

Tomorrow, Strega Nona thought, *I'll send* regali—*presents*—to Bambolona and Big Anthony.

The day the presents arrived, Big Anthony was outside feeding the goat.
Bambolona couldn't wait. She opened them and found seashore candy
for Big Anthony and bubble bath for her.

I want the candy! Bambolona thought. Quickly she switched the tags.

Big Anthony opened his present. "Bambolona, what *is* bubble bath?"
"You put it in your bathwater and it makes lots of bubbles. It's very
nice," Bambolona said, chewing on her candy.

124

"Oh, no!" the Mayor shouted. "*Non ancora!* NOT AGAIN!"

"At least it's not pasta!" Big Anthony shouted, sailing by on the bubbles.

At the seashore, a dove flew in with a message for Strega Nona. "Bambolona," Strega Nona said to herself. "What have you done?"

"Well, Strega Nona," the Mayor announced, "at least the village will be *molto pulito*—very clean! No real harm done."

"Except when the wrong present gets into the wrong hands," Strega Nona said. "I hope that YOU have learned your lesson, Bambolona!"

"*Mi dispiace*, Strega Nona, I'm sorry." Bambolona said.

"Me too!" Big Anthony said.

"But Strega Nona, this means that you'll never be able to take a vacation," the Mayor said.

"*Certo!*" Strega Nona answered. "Oh, yes, I will. Next time, I'll just take Big Anthony and Bambolona with me!"

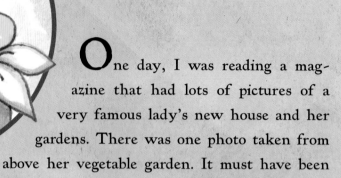

One day, I was reading a magazine that had lots of pictures of a very famous lady's new house and her gardens. There was one photo taken from above her vegetable garden. It must have been taken from a helicopter. It was so neat and orderly. All the vegetables were planted in very precise rows, one after the other. "Just like my garden," I thought I heard Strega Nona whisper. That's when I got the idea for *Strega Nona's Harvest*.

I wonder, I thought, *what would Big Anthony's garden look like?*

I remembered that a long time ago, when I lived in Vermont, I made a vegetable garden—well, really a RADISH garden. Instead of planting a row or two of seeds every few days, I planted all the seeds at once.

Of course, all the radishes came up together, so I had more radishes than I knew what to do with. I drove around giving bunches of radishes to everyone I knew. A similar thing happens here in New Hampshire, where I live now, but with zucchini. I don't grow zucchini or any other vegetables anymore, but it's not unusual to find a bag of zucchini outside your door from the neighbors who grow it.

My radish garden of long ago looked like a mess when all the radishes came up. *That's what Big Anthony's garden would be like!* I thought. So that's how I drew it in the book.

Tomie dePaola

Strega Nona's HARVEST

For Greg and all the fine folks
at Spring Ledge Farm

It was spring, and all the snow had melted. The rich earth was beginning to warm. Strega Nona pulled out a small wooden box that had been hidden away in the dark cupboard all winter.

"Aha," she said as she took out small packets of seeds she had saved from last year's garden. "*Qui siete, i miei amici piccoli*—here you are, my little friends."

"Why were all those seeds in the dark, Strega Nona?" Big Anthony asked.

"Well, *mio caro*—my dear," Strega Nona answered, "they had to rest, just like you do, so they will be able to do their job when we plant them in the garden."

"When will we plant them, Strega Nona?" Bambolona asked.

"When *la luna*—the moon—tells us, Bambolona. Then we will plant each kind of seed carefully in the right place. After all, we can't just throw the seeds into the ground in a big pile! A garden must be orderly so it is easy to pick the vegetables."

"Now, let me look in my *libro di giardino*—Garden Book—to see what we did last year."

Every year, Strega Nona wrote down in her book what she planted, when and where. She never put the same vegetables in the same spot.

"We have to move them around," she told her young helpers, "so the soil will stay happy and strong. But first, Anthony, you must spread the compost and manure we saved all winter and rake it into the soil so our vegetables will grow as big and beautiful as can be."

So, Big Anthony put a clothespin on his nose and did his job.

"Children, come," called Strega Nona. "It is almost the end of *Maggio*—May—and there will be a full moon tonight. It is time to plant. Now, Anthony, I want you to make nice straight rows in the soil with the end of the hoe. That's where the seeds will go."

"Big Anthony," Bambolona scolded, "you're not making the rows straight enough. You know that Strega Nona likes everything Perfect!" She added, "And so do I!"

Bambolona is so bossy, Big Anthony thought. *Someday, I'll show her I can do something perfect, too.*

That night, when the full moon rose in the sky, Strega Nona quietly crept out to the garden. She looked up at the moon and sang:

O *Bella Luna*, smile on me,

And on the seeds I sow,

And let the moonbeams shine from thee,

To make my garden grow.

"And now for the *ingrediente segreto*—secret ingredient."

Strega Nona blew three kisses to the moon.

"Oh," said Big Anthony as he watched her. Suddenly he spied some seeds that had dropped on the ground. "I know. I'll plant my OWN *perfect* garden behind the goat shed. I'll *show* Bambolona!"

So, Big Anthony poked some holes in the ground. He threw in the seeds and covered them with compost and manure. He watered and watered.

Then he sang Strega Nona's song:

    O *Bella Luna*, smile on me,

    And on the seeds I sow,

    And let the moonbeams shine from thee,

    To make my garden *really* grow.

He blew the three kisses to the moon. And just to be sure, he blew three more.

As it did every year, Strega Nona's garden grew beautifully.

Big Anthony's garden   *Strega Nona's garden*

Soon, bright green *insalata*—salad—was on the table.

Fresh peas were added to the pasta from Strega Nona's pasta pot.

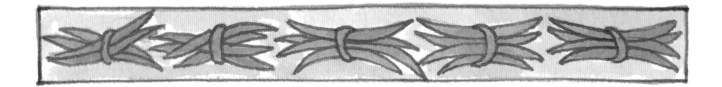

Green beans were cooked in olive oil.

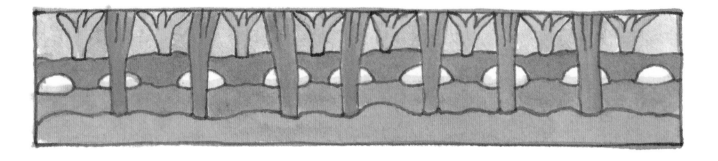

And the other vegetables were growing beautifully, too.

Big Anthony's secret garden was growing as well.
But not quite so beautifully. It looked like a jungle!

Mamma mia, Big Anthony thought. *I can't let
Bambolona—or Strega Nona—see this mess!*

Big Anthony's garden   Strega Nona's garden

Now it was time to harvest the vegetables that Strega Nona would keep over the winter.

It wasn't long before the root cellar and the rafters in the kitchen were full.
"*Molto bene*—very good!" said Strega Nona to Bambolona and
Big Anthony. "A job well done. We all deserve a good rest."

But Big Anthony didn't have time to rest. He had other work to do.

"I've got to pick all my vegetables. What will I do with them?" he said.

The next morning, when Strega Nona opened her door,
she found a big pile of vegetables.

"*Santo cielo*—good heavens," Strega Nona said.
"Where did these come from?"

She called Big Anthony and Bambolona. "My children, please carry all these vegetables into the kitchen. *Grazie*—thank you."

Every morning there were more vegetables outside the door.
Soon, there was hardly any room to move in the kitchen.

Maybe these are from the villagers, Strega Nona thought. Perhaps they had too good of a harvest. Well, I must find out—and soon. If this goes on, I won't have room to sleep in my little bed at night!

The next morning, Strega Nona packed a basket of vegetables. "I'll take these to the Sisters at the convent and maybe they'll know something."

"Oh, *grazie*, Strega Nona," the Mother Superior said. "You must have heard our prayers. Our garden didn't do well this season. In fact, no one's garden in the village did. We had too much rain down here, while you had lots of sun on your hill."

So Strega Nona went right to the mayor.

"Sì—yes, Strega Nona," Signor Mayor said. "The harvest was poor
this year."

"Well, I have more than enough to share," Strega Nona said. "I will have
a Harvest Feast tomorrow evening at sundown. Tell everyone to come."

And Strega Nona practically ran up to her little house.

"Bambolona, Big Anthony, come quickly," Strega Nona said. "We have much work to do. I am going to have a Harvest Feast for all our friends and neighbors. We shall share our bounty!"

"*Evviva, evviva*—hurrah, hurrah for Strega Nona!" everyone shouted.

"*Arrivederci, buonanotte*—good-bye, good night,"
Strega Nona and her two helpers called out.

Strega Nona looked around at her empty kitchen. "Well, that took care of that," she said with a smile. "But I still wonder where all those vegetables came from." And she climbed into bed.

Later that night . . .

I love to read cookbooks. One of my favorite cookbooks is by my friend Carol Field. It's called *Celebrating Italy*. Carol and her husband spent a lot of time traveling to lots of little towns and villages for the different feast days that are held throughout the year.

Of course, in the olden times when Strega Nona lived, all the people would have celebrated many of the same feasts, especially during Advent, the time before Christmas, Christmas itself, and then the days up to Epiphany on January 6.

And in Italy, every feast has its own special food. I got really hungry doing THIS book. Enjoy, and as *my* Italian grandmother always said, *"Mangia, mangia!"* ("Eat, eat!!")

Tomie dePaola
Strega Nona's Gift

For Zoe, Gina, Jarrett
and of course Ralph.

Everyone in the little village in Calabria, including Strega Nona, had been busy in their kitchens and at their tables since the month of December began.

First was the Feast of San Nicola – Saint Nicholas – on December 6. The children got to choose the food for this feast because San Nicola was said to love children.

The next feast was on December 13: the Feast of Santa Lucia – Saint Lucy. In her honor, a special pudding was made with soft wheat berries and ricotta cheese.

As the weeks went by, Strega Nona kept Big Anthony very busy with errands.

When Bambolona had to go back into the village to help her father,
Papa Bambo, at the bakery, Big Anthony had an idea.

"Strega Nona," Big Anthony said, "since Bambolona isn't here,
I'm ready to help you in the kitchen!"

"Oh," Strega Nona replied, "that is very nice of you, Big Anthony, but I can manage just fine. Besides, you have plenty to do."

"You know," Big Anthony said with a smile, "you're right, Strega Nona."

That was a close one, thought Strega Nona.

December 24 was La Vigilia – Christmas Eve. Every house in the village was cooking fish for the Feast of the Seven Fishes.

There was no meat served on Christmas Eve, and no meat was eaten until after the midnight mass.

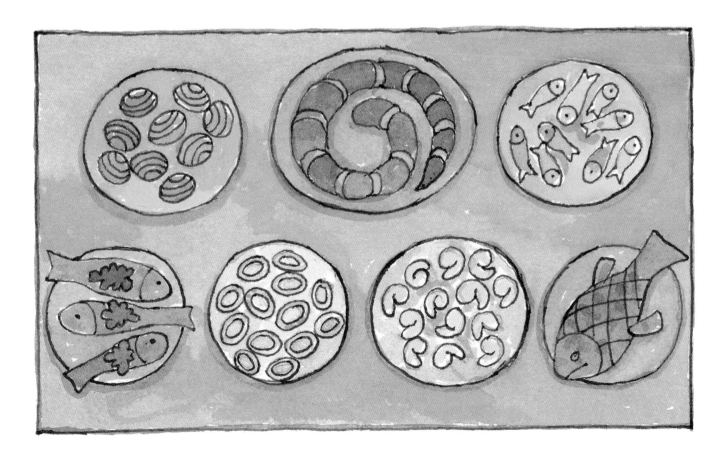

After the mass, everyone climbed the little hill to Strega Nona's
for her annual Christmas Feast.

There were tables and tables of food.

The Zampognari – shepherds from Abruzzi – were there to sing.
The villagers and the children danced under the stars to celebrate
the birth of baby Jesus.

As a rosy light appeared in the sky, everyone went home for a good, big sleep. After all, there was still a whole week of *festas* left.

On December 31, New Year's Eve, was the Feast of San Silvestro – Saint Sylvester.

"Big Anthony," Strega Nona said, "you must eat your lentils and rice pudding. You won't be prosperous next year if you don't."

"Strega Nona," Big Anthony asked, "will it be all right if I go down to the village to watch the New Year Bonfire? Everyone will be there."

"Of course, *caro*. Only be very careful when the church bell rings at midnight. Hide in a doorway or under an archway. You know that people throw old things they no longer want out the windows. I heard that Signora Anita threw her old stove last year. It nearly killed Signore Mayor."

"I'll be careful," Big Anthony promised.

"Oh, and don't forget to wear your RED underwear. Everyone has to wear their red underwear for *capodanno* – New Year. It brings good luck."

On January 5, the eve of Epifania – Epiphany, the Feast of the Three Kings – once again everyone was cooking. But this time for their animals.

There was a legend that at midnight on the Eve of Epiphany all the animals could speak to each other. It was because the ox and the donkey kept the baby Jesus warm with their breath in the manger.

So, the villagers wanted to give their animals a feast. No one wanted their animals gossiping with each other about how poorly fed or mistreated they were.

Strega Nona was cooking wonderful dishes for her rabbit, her peacock, her dove and especially her goat.

Delicious smells that came out of the kitchen nearly drove Big Anthony crazy. So, when Strega Nona called him in for supper, he almost knocked the door down.

But there at his place at the table was a plain dish of pasta from Strega Nona's pasta pot. On the counter were four dishes that looked and smelled so, so good.

"What are those dishes?" Big Anthony asked.

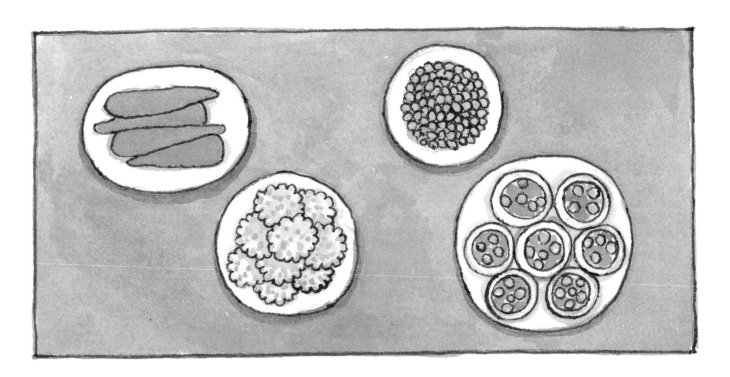

"Those are special dishes for the animals. It's a special night for them.
There are carrots for the rabbit, corn cakes for the peacock, sweet seeds
for the dove, and turnips stuffed with greens and *ceci* for the goat. As soon
as you finish your pasta, take Signora Goat's dish out to her, please."

Big Anthony stopped outside the goat shed. "I'll just take a tiny taste."

"Oh, that's so good," said Big Anthony as he tasted more and more.

"*Santo cielo* – it's all gone!" cried Big Anthony as he looked down
at the empty plate.

He quickly filled the plate with hay and oats and left it at
the window of the goat shed and quietly ran away.

As Strega Nona tidied up her kitchen, she thought of all the villagers and how they had all worked so hard for their animals all day. And how they probably all had simple suppers like she and Big Anthony.

"I will give everyone a gift," she said as she opened her ancient book.

"I will give everyone a wonderful dream. A dream about food!"

And sure enough, as each one of the villagers drifted off to sleep, everything seemed to turn to food. The fountain poured out milk and honey. The walls turned into ricotta and mozzarella. Bedposts became sausages and the bedsheets changed into sheets of lasagna.

While the villagers were sleeping, the animals gathered in the square
to tell each other what amazing food they had been given that night.

"The sisters gave us the most delicious fried fish," said the cats from
the convent. "What did Strega Nona give you, Signora Goat?"

"I don't know. Big Anthony ate it all before I even had a look at it."

"That's terrible," said the Mayor's dog. "What did you do?"

"I ate his blanket," Signora Goat answered. "I'll bet he's so cold that he doesn't sleep all night."

And Big Anthony didn't sleep. And because he didn't sleep,
he didn't dream about all the wonderful food.

He was not only cold. He was very hungry!

The next morning, the Day of Epiphany, everyone except Big Anthony had full stomachs from the dream they received from Strega Nona.

In the early afternoon everyone gathered once again at
Strega Nona's house to celebrate the Feast of Epiphany.

First, everyone took a piece of cake. Whoever had the piece that had a fava bean in it became the king or the queen of the Feast.

"Hurray, look!" some of the men shouted. "It's Big Anthony!"

They carried King Anthony around the table on their shoulders and sat him down in the special chair.

"Well, Big Anthony, because you are king and the Three Kings brought gifts to the child Jesus, what would you like for a gift?" Strega Nona asked.

"A new blanket," Big Anthony answered. "And," he added, "some of that delicious turnip dish you made for Signora Goat last night!"

"Pronto," said Strega Nona.

"Here you are, King Anthony," Strega Nona said. "And *buonanotte.*"

"*Grazie,* Strega Nona," said Big Anthony. "Thank you."

Then Big Anthony wrapped himself in his new blanket
and knocked on Signora Goat's window.

He held out the dish of turnips. "Let's have a truce," he said.

And *presto*. The holiday season was over for another year.

Buone Feste—Happy Holidays!

December 6: Feast of San Nicola

Saint Nicholas, a bishop in the third century, was known for his generosity and love of children. He is also the inspiration for *Babbo Natale* (Father Christmas). On his feast, children are allowed to choose their favorite meal.

December 13: Feast of Santa Lucia

Saint Lucy lived in Sicily in the third century. Legend states that she was blinded for her faith, but God restored her sight. To honor Saint Lucy, a dish called *cuccia*, made with ricotta, sugar and boiled whole wheat berries, is eaten on her feast.

December 24: Feast of La Vigilia—Christmas Eve

This feast on *La Vigilia* commemorates the wait for the baby Jesus's midnight birth (*Vigilia di Natale*). No meat is allowed, so to this day the tradition is to eat seven courses of seafood, including eel and *baccalà*.

December 25: Christmas

Natale, Italian for "Christmas," is literally "birthday"—and this feast celebrates the birthday of *Gesù Bambino* (baby Jesus, or the Christ child). It is traditionally held after the midnight mass, and meats of all sorts are served.

December 31: The Feast of San Silvestro

Saint Sylvester was a fourth-century pope whose feast day is on New Year's Eve. Lentils and slices of sausage are eaten because they look like coins and symbolize good fortune and the richness of life for the coming year.

January 1: Il Capodanno— New Year's Day

Il Capodanno translates to "the top of the year," and on this day Italians wear red underwear for good luck and gather together for a huge dinner.

January 5: The Eve of Epifania—Epiphany

According to legend, this is a special night when animals can talk, so their owners are sure to feed them well. In the Calabria region of Italy, it is also said that on this night, rivers and fountains run with wine and olive oil.

January 6: Feast of Epifania—Epiphany

This feast commemorates the arrival of the Magi, the three wise men who brought gifts to the infant Jesus, and often includes a special "Kings' Cake." According to tradition, the cake contains a bean, and the person who finds it rules the feast. This day ends the holiday season.

To learn more about the feasts of Italy, see Carol Field's book *Celebrating Italy*.

RECIPES AND COOKING TIPS FROM TOMIE

QUANTO BASTA!

None of us has a magic pasta pot like Strega Nona does. At least I don't.

But I did have an Italian grandmother who was a wonderful cook, and tasty food always came out of her kitchen.

When I asked her for her recipes, I was introduced to the art of Nana Fall-River's cooking: no recipes, no measurements, just "quanto basta"—as much as you need or as much as you want. So in the same spirit, the following suggestions for good Italian things to make and eat are presented to you "quanto basta." This is all about using what you have and making a dish to your own taste.

*A WORD TO YOUNG READERS—
please do not try any of these good things without
a grown-up to help and guide you.

BRUSCHETTA

A simple Italian appetizer

bruschetta

Making the toast:

- Preheat the oven to 350°F.

- Start with a good loaf of French or Italian bread.

- Cut into half inch thick slices and place on a baking sheet.

- Drizzle with extra-virgin olive oil.

- Bake for 10-15 minutes.

- Remove from oven and immediately rub each slice with a clove of garlic and sprinkle lightly with sea salt.

HERE ARE A FEW SUGGESTED TOPPINGS—
there are as many more as your imagination will allow!

Fresh tomatoes, diced and tossed with salt, pepper and torn basil leaves, and drizzled with olive oil.

Fresh mozzarella, sliced and drizzled with olive oil, sprinkled with chopped capers and parsley.

Canned cannellini beans rinsed and drained, then mashed with finely chopped garlic, olive oil, a sprinkle of salt, and a few red pepper flakes.

Spread with any of the many excellent tapenades available in the gourmet section of the market.

Now you're on your own. Have fun, and MANGIA!

basil

PASTA

There are basically two kinds of pasta:

DRIED—such as spaghetti, fusilli, shells, elbows and many other shapes and variations.

pasta

FRESH—which is often made with the addition of eggs. Some fresh types of pasta include many of the shapes above, as well as favorites like fettuccine and pappardelle.

Dried pasta can be found in supermarkets and specialty stores packaged in boxes or bags.

Fresh pasta can also be found in these markets and stores, usually in the dairy counter. Fresh pasta can also be made at home.

Another type of pasta is stuffed pasta, such as tortellini and the most popular, ravioli. These can come in dried or fresh versions, too.

TIPS FOR COOKING PASTA

DRIED pasta should be cooked according to directions on package—about two ounces (or more) per serving.

It should be cooked in plenty of well-salted water. My Italian grandmother always said that the pasta water should be "salty like the sea."

Never add oil to the water—enough water is the secret to keep pasta from sticking to itself.

dried pasta

Once cooked to your taste, pasta can be drained in a colander or scooped out of the water with tongs or a "spider," a special type of screened ladle.

TIPS FOR MIXING PASTA WITH THE TOPPINGS

Prepare your sauce or topping while pasta cooks, in a large sauté pan or bowl that is big enough to hold pasta and sauce.

Many Italian cooks pour the cooked, drained pasta into the pan and cook it a bit more. This way the pasta will absorb all the flavors. This is better than pouring the sauce on the pasta.

Another Italian secret is to reserve a cup of cooking water to add in case you need to adjust the consistency of the sauce.

FRESH pasta is also cooked in boiling water that has been generously salted.

However, it only takes a few minutes to cook so start testing for doneness about 1 to 2 minutes after the water comes back to a boil.

fresh pasta

There is NO remedy for overcooked pasta except to mash it up and use it for wallpaper paste.

PASTA SAUCES

Cook pasta according to directions and number of servings.

SIMPLE BREAD CRUMB SAUCE

(I like dried angel hair or spaghetti)

Extra-virgin olive oil

Butter at room temperature

Reserved, hot pasta water, about a cup

*Garlic—a few cloves finely chopped
(or dried garlic flakes)*

Bread crumbs

Parmesan or other grated cheese

*Optional: chopped parsley,
red pepper flakes*

garlic

- Put about a tablespoon of olive oil and lump of butter in individual serving bowls. Add garlic and mash mixture. If using pepper flakes, add now.

- When pasta is cooked, drain quickly. Reserve one cup of hot pasta water.

- Add pasta serving to each bowl. Toss lightly.

- Add a few spoonfuls of pasta water. Toss.

- Top with a generous helping of bread crumbs and a drizzle of olive oil, cheese and, if using, parsley. Toss one more time and serve.

UNCOOKED TOMATO SAUCE

(I like dried spaghetti or spaghettini for these)

*Tomatoes—either fresh grape, cherry,
or plum tomatoes OR canned
San Marzano whole peeled tomatoes,
drained*

Extra-virgin olive oil

Pinch of sugar

Basil leaves (torn)

Parmesan or other grated cheese

- Chop, slice, or "squish" tomatoes in the serving bowl.

- Drizzle with olive oil.

- Add pinch of sugar.

- Add pasta. Toss.

- Sprinkle with basil and cheese. Toss again and serve.

tomatoes

BASIC CREAM SAUCE

(I like to serve this with fresh pasta)

(For Four Servings)

1 cup heavy cream (try not to use ultra-pasteurized unless that's the only kind you can get)

4 tablespoons butter
Pinch of salt
Pinch of fresh nutmeg

- Melt butter in a large sauté pan.

- Add cream and bring to a boil.

- Lower heat and stir with a heat-proof spatula until cream reduces to about half its original volume.

- Add pinch of salt and nutmeg.

- You are now ready to serve. You could also add other ingredients to make these variations.

lemon

Lemon Cream Sauce:

- Add lemon juice and grated zest as cream begins to boil.

- Add cooked pasta to pan and toss.

Mushroom Cream Sauce:

- Sauté mushrooms in butter and olive oil.

- Add to cream as it reduces.

- Add cooked pasta to pan and toss.

- Serve with grated cheese.

cream

Tomato Cream Sauce

- Diced fresh or drained canned tomatoes.

- Add to cream as it reduces.

- Add a pinch of sugar and salt.

- Add cooked pasta to pan and bring to a boil.

- Serve with grated cheese.

Experiment,
and remember,
QUANTO BASTA!

parsley

A SIMPLE SOUP
This makes a nice lunch or start to your dinner.

You will need:

Good quality chicken, beef, or vegetable broth.
Allow approximately 2 cups (16 ounces) for 2 small servings.
(Most cans contain about 2 cups.)

For each cup of broth, measure about a <u>quarter</u> cup
of pastina (little pasta) or orzo.

Bring broth to a boil, add pastina or orzo,
lower to a simmer and cook until al dente
or to your taste—about 8 to 10 minutes.

Sprinkle with sea salt and freshly ground pepper, and, if you'd like,
fresh parsley or torn basil leaves and a drizzle of olive oil.

Top it off with freshly grated Parmesan cheese.

Parmesan cheese

TOMIE'S SALAD

Salad is usually served after the main course at a traditional Italian dinner.

The best tomatoes from your garden or market

Extra-virgin olive oil

Balsamic vinegar

Burrata cheese, if you can find it— or fresh mozzarella or ricotta cheese

Salad greens

olive oil

- Line a plate or bowl with greens, top with pieces of tomato. Place cheese on top of tomatoes.

- Sprinkle lightly with sea salt and freshly ground pepper and a light drizzle of olive oil and balsamic vinegar.

- Optional: Sprinkle with torn basil, parsley, fresh tarragon if desired, and enjoy!

basil

tomatoes

STREGA NONA'S LITTLE NIGHT SONG

The sun is low up in the sky
The shepherd finds a sheep gone astray
While the birds fly back to their nests
And the children stop their play

The sun sets up in the sky
The twilight approaches to conquer the day
As an owl hoots, the children are eating
The daylight fades away

A star twinkles bright up in the sky
Lights in the window appear
Crickets chirp while the animals snuggle up
The children say their prayers; bedtime is near

The silver moon begins to shine
A nightingale sings to the fireflies
Sleep falls over the children
They close their eyes

STREGA NONA'S LITTLE NIGHT SONG
Una Piccola Serenata della Strega Nona

Music by William Ögmundson
Lyrics by Tomie dePaola and William Ögmundson

Lento

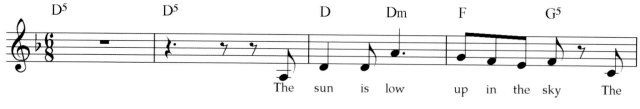

The sun is low up in the sky The

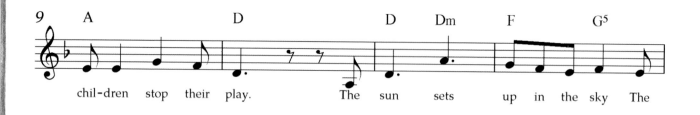

shep-herd finds a sheep gone a-stray While the birds fly back to their nests and the

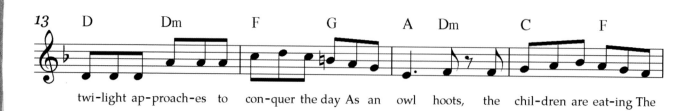

chil-dren stop their play. The sun sets up in the sky The

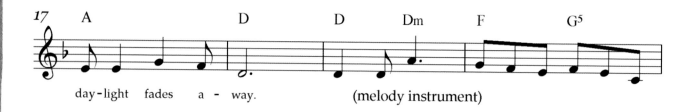

twi-light ap-proach-es to con-quer the day As an owl hoots, the chil-dren are eat-ing The

day-light fades a - way. (melody instrument)

A star twin-kles bright up in the sky

Lights in the win-dow ap - pear Crick-ets chirp while the an - i-mals snug-gle up The

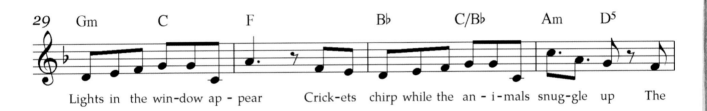

chil - dren say their prayers; bed-time is near. The

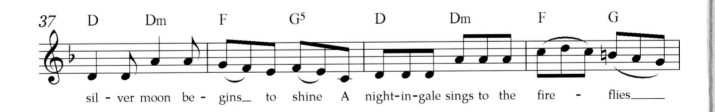

sil - ver moon be - gins_ to shine A night-in-gale sings to the fire - flies_____

Sleep falls ov - er the chil - dren They close their____ eyes.

TOMIE DEPAOLA

was born in Meriden, Connecticut, in 1934 to a family of Irish and Italian background. At the age of four, he said: "I'm going to be an artist. I'm going to write stories and draw pictures for books." His determination led to a BFA from Pratt Institute in Brooklyn, New York, and an MFA from the California College of Arts & Crafts in Oakland, California, and to illustrating his first children's book in 1965.

Now one of the world's most prolific and popular children's authors and illustrators, Tomie has illustrated over 250 books and written the stories for half of them. Many of his childhood experiences are recounted in his Fairmount Avenue Books, including the first one, *26 Fairmount Avenue*, which won a Newbery Honor Award. Tomie also won a Caldecott Honor Award for *Strega Nona*.

Tomie has also received many other awards, including the Smithson Medal, the University of Minnesota's Kerlan Award, the Catholic Library Association's Regina Medal, and the Laura Ingalls Wilder Award for his "substantial and lasting contribution to literature for children." The committee noted his "innate understanding of childhood, distinctive visual style, and remarkable ability to adapt his voice to perfectly suit the story." It called Strega Nona, the wise Grandma Witch, "an enduring character who has charmed generations of children."

Today, Tomie works in a renovated two-hundred-year-old barn in New London, New Hampshire, with his Airedale terrier, Brontë. To show how beloved he is in that state, the New Hampshire State Council on the Arts designated him a Living Treasure.

To learn more about this extraordinary man, read *Tomie dePaola: His Art & His Stories*, which was written by Barbara Elleman and provides both a biography of dePaola and a detailed analysis of his work.